KEEPER OF THE CRYSTALS

Eve and the Last Dragon

For Fergus. Thank you for everything.

First published in the UK in 2017
by New Frontier Publishing Pty Ltd
93 Harbord Street, London SW6 6PN
www.newfrontierpublishing.co.uk

ISBN: 978-1-912076-66-6 (PB)

A CIP catalogue record for this book is available from
the British Library.

Cover illustration and design by Celeste Hulme

Printed in China
10 9 8 7 6 5 4 3 2 1

KEEPER OF THE CRYSTALS

Eve and the Last Dragon

Jess Black
Illustrated by Celeste Hulme

WICKLOW COUNTY COUNCIL
LIBRARY SERVICE

Eve gazed out at the ever-changing Australian bush whizzing past her window. Dry tussocks of grass were dwarfed by the tall eucalypt and banksia trees.

Eve usually enjoyed this view and the gentle rocking of the train, but not today. Eve was on edge. Her stomach was twisted into a tight knot and she was finding it hard

to keep still. Her hands were clammy and her mouth felt dry.

Eve had taken the train alone to her gran's house many times. Her mum would see her onto the train and Sylvie would be waiting for her on the platform at Marigold Station. Eve's heart raced at the thought.

Sylvie had told Eve it was time to open the box Eve had been forbidden to touch. This ancient box would take them back into a world where dark magic ruled. The last time Sylvie had been there she had been lucky to escape alive. Eve felt sure that her grandmother was afraid.

'Come on, Eve.' She steeled herself. 'Get a grip.'

Eve's body rocked to the right as the train rattled around the final bend before slowing down in its approach to Marigold. Then, swinging her backpack over her shoulder,

she made her way down the aisle towards the automatic doors. The train drew to a halt and after a hiss of brakes the doors slid open.

Eve stepped onto the platform. She glanced around at the people gathered at the station. Sylvie's neighbour was there, and the lady who ran the fruit shop, but there was no sign of Sylvie. As the crowd quickly dispersed, Eve found herself looking at a familiar face.

'What are *you* doing here?' Eve asked the boy standing in front of her. She dropped her heavy backpack onto the ground at her feet.

'Nice to see you too!' Oscar fired back with a hint of irritation. 'I'm really well – thanks for asking.'

Eve scowled. 'I don't need to be picked up! I can walk to Gran's house on my own.'

'You're welcome. I love spending my afternoons waiting at train stations for grumpy girls.' Oscar pointed to Eve's backpack. 'And carrying their bags.'

Eve crossed her arms. 'Just because I'm a girl it doesn't mean I can't carry my own bag.'

'Fine,' Oscar snapped.

'Fine,' Eve muttered, then let out a deep sigh. They were both acting like toddlers. 'Oscar, where's Gran?'

'No idea,' Oscar shrugged. 'She came over to my place this morning and asked me to meet you.'

Eve's mind raced. Sylvie might be old but she wouldn't have missed picking Eve up from the train for anything. And why didn't she tell Eve that she was sending Oscar? It didn't make sense.

'She's up to something.' Eve began to

pace back and forth on the platform. Oscar glanced down at the backpack on the ground in front of him.

'I'm not picking it up,' he said stubbornly, hands on hips.

'What's going on?' Eve continued, half talking to herself. 'She's had me all riled up about this box and now she's done a vanishing act!' She halted suddenly as a thought struck her. 'Wait a minute! She'd better not have –'

'I'm just making it clear that I'm not carrying that bag,' Oscar interrupted, glaring at Eve. 'You were very rude to me.'

'She wouldn't!' Eve took off in the direction of the station exit.

'Eve!' Oscar called after her. Eve broke into a run.

'Come on, Oscar!' she called over her shoulder. She saw Oscar nudge the backpack

with his foot, then swing it over his shoulder. She waited impatiently as he caught up.

'I have a bad feeling about this,' Oscar muttered.

*E*ve's fingers searched for the key that her gran kept tucked under the large earthenware pot at the side of the house. 'Gotcha.' Her fingers grasped the smooth metal buried in the soil.

She let herself in through the front door and was greeted by the loud ticking of the grandfather clock in the hall.

'Gran!' Eve called. She paused in the hall

and listened. Nothing. She headed straight for Sylvie's bedroom. The room was empty and the curtains were drawn. Sylvie's bed was made, the white linen neatly smoothed across the surface of the bed.

'What are you up to, Gran?' Eve whispered as she searched the room for clues. The room offered no answers. She spun around and nearly collided with Oscar.

'Watch it!' Eve barked at him.

Oscar glared at her but bit his tongue. He huffed and dropped the backpack on the floor. Then he looked at the tears in Eve's eyes and his manner softened.

'Should we call the police?'

Eve shook her head and slumped onto the bed. 'And tell them what? That my grandmother, who has magical powers and can enter other worlds to save mythical creatures, has gone missing?'

'Well, when you put it like that …' Oscar sat on the bed next to Eve.

'Just give me a moment to think,' Eve snapped.

'Okay, Eve. Peace. I just want to help – I care about Sylvie too.'

'I know. I'm sorry,' Eve said tearfully. 'I was going to tell you everything when I got here and I've been horrible instead.'

'Just don't cry,' said Oscar with a small smile. 'I can cope with anything except you crying.'

Eve giggled. 'Agreed. No crying.' She wiped her eyes with the back of her hand and took a deep breath. 'Gran wanted me to go into another world with her. The world you can only go to when you open the Chinese box with the dragons on the lid. Remember we saw it in the attic, and Gran said that it had powerful magic in it?'

Oscar nodded.

'Last time I was here, Gran said we both needed to go into that world. She said the magic was so dark that she couldn't do it alone,' Eve continued. 'She also said that time was running out and it needed to be done now. That's why I'm here during term time.'

'I thought it was strange when your gran asked me to meet you today,' Oscar said thoughtfully.

Suddenly Eve realised what her grandmother had done. 'Sylvie's gone without me!' she blurted out.

'Why would she do that?' Oscar asked.

'I don't know. It doesn't make any sense.'

'Since when does anything you and your gran do make sense?' asked Oscar wryly.

Eve leaped up. 'We have to go, Oscar.'

'Wait,' he said quickly. Eve saw him grab

10

a piece of blank paper from Sylvie's writing desk and scribble a note: *We've gone looking for you. Oscar and Eve.*

***

Eve and Oscar climbed the steep ladder that led into the attic space. The attic door was ajar and Eve could see the small brass key sticking out of the lock.

'She's been in the attic alright.'

Eve pushed the door open and stepped into the darkness. She'd come prepared and turned on the large torch her gran kept handy in case of blackouts.

'See anything?' Oscar called from the ladder.

Eve shone the beam around the small space but there was no sign of Sylvie.

'She's not here,' Eve answered.

A flash of red caught Eve's eye and she held the beam of light on the Chinese lacquered box. Oscar climbed up and stood beside her.

'Remember the last time we were up here?' he asked her.

Eve nodded. It seemed so long ago now. Eve and Oscar had been exploring the attic when Eve had stumbled upon a crystal figurine of a unicorn. As soon as she had touched the crystal an ancient magic was unleashed and Eve and Oscar were transported to the desert of Panthor. They had helped save the unicorn and the people of the desert. Since then they had visited more worlds and had many other adventures. Eve now understood more about her gift as a crystal keeper. She and her gran had the same magic inside them – a magic that connected them to ancient and

mythical creatures who needed their help.

The Chinese box was about the size of a shoebox. It was covered in vivid red and gold images of dragons. Eve kneeled down in front of the box and handed Oscar the torch. She slowly undid the small gold latch and opened the lid.

Inside lay a single piece of paper. Eve recognised the handwriting immediately. She read aloud: *I have been called urgently into another world. You will need to go to Xeria without me. You are ready for this, Eve. You have Oscar. Good luck. Gran.*

'I can't believe she wants me to go there alone!' Eve shook her head in disbelief.

'She says you have me. What am I? Chopped liver? Your gran trusts me. Sometimes I think you don't appreciate my talents ...' Oscar trailed off as Eve silenced him with a look. 'I'll stop talking now.'

Under the note lay a thick black velvet cloth. Eve lifted the material and a ray of brilliant golden light streamed out. Both Eve and Oscar had to shield their eyes and look away. Once her eyes had adjusted to the bright light Eve peered inside again. Lying in the bottom of the box was a small crystal in the shape of a dragon. Eve felt the familiar rush of energy – first in her fingers and hands, then spreading fast through her whole body.

'You ready for this?' Eve asked Oscar.

'Ready as I'll ever be,' Oscar replied as he grabbed Eve's arm firmly.

Eve picked up the crystal but flinched and dropped it back into the box, feeling as if she had been burned.

'The magic is different. Stronger.' Eve rubbed her palm. It felt hot and it throbbed.

'You can do this, Eve.' Oscar gave her a

smile of encouragement.

Eve picked up the crystal again and grimaced but held it in her palm. All of a sudden Eve and Oscar were completely surrounded by a wall of flame.

'Fire!' Oscar tried to shield Eve from the flames with his body.

The heat was unbearable. The flames danced around Eve and Oscar, bright hot flickers of red and yellow with tinges of green. Eve felt her face burn up and the bare skin on her arms and legs prickled in the heat.

Oscar broke into a coughing fit. Eve

looked down and saw a thick cloud of dark smoke around their feet. Her eyes stung so much that tears poured down her face.

'We have to get out of here.' Eve knew that smoke could be even more deadly than flames. She grabbed Oscar's hand and made her way to the attic door. But the fire had beaten them to it and the exit was completely cut off. Eve gazed around in a panic. The attic had no windows and they had very little time.

'There!' Eve noticed an old air vent in the back wall. It was a small circular shape but looked about the right size for her and Oscar to squeeze through.

'Quick!' Oscar coughed again. He looked pale in the light from the flames – too pale. Eve pulled him over to the vent. They wrenched off the metal cover and inhaled the fresh air from outside.

17

Eve looked down and gasped. Instead of seeing her gran's garden and Oscar's house next door she saw endless rolling green hills. There were no buildings in sight.

'Xeria,' Eve whispered.

'Hurry, Eve. You go first.'

Oscar gave Eve a hoist up. She easily stuck her head and shoulders through the gap and then pulled her legs out. Once outside Eve realised she was on the top of an enormous stone building. There was a small ledge that gave her just enough room to gain a foothold.

Eve reached inside to take Oscar's hand and help him out. The gap was small but with lots of grunting she managed to pull Oscar through.

The pair flattened themselves against the wall and took in their surroundings. Gradually her eyes cleared up and Eve could

see properly. The air cooled her skin. 'We're on top of some kind of castle,' she observed.

'And we need to get off this ledge,' Oscar said through clenched teeth. Eve looked at him and saw his eyes were screwed shut.

'Did the smoke hurt your eyes?' she asked.

Oscar cleared his throat and opened an eye. 'I'm afraid of heights,' he admitted.

It was a long way down to the ground. Even Eve felt a little scared. She took Oscar's hand to steady him. 'Whatever you do, don't look down,' Eve commanded. 'Look at my face and in next to no time we'll be off this wall.'

Oscar nodded woozily and stared helplessly into Eve's eyes as they shimmied along the narrow ledge. After what seemed like an age they were standing safely inside the low wall of the top turret.

'You can let go of me now,' Eve said to

Oscar with a doubtful smile. She wasn't used to seeing her friend out of his comfort zone.

'Let's get out of here,' he replied shakily. 'I want to be standing on solid ground.' A staircase wound down in a spiral from the turret.

'Lead the way,' said Eve.

Oscar couldn't get down the steps fast enough and took them two at a time.

Eve glanced at the hand that had been holding the dragon crystal. As she had expected, the lines on her palm had rearranged themselves into a perfect dragon. Eve knew that this meant the dragon needed her help.

After climbing down the steps, the pair found themselves in a dark and musty stone corridor that was thick with cobwebs. There was a faint smell of smoke from the

fire but the danger they now faced was being trapped inside the castle with no way of escape. Each corridor they entered appeared to be completely empty, and every room they passed had wooden boards over its windows.

'Finally!' Oscar breathed. Eve looked over his shoulder and was relieved to see an open doorway leading out of the castle. They wasted no time in heading towards it.

As the pair approached the threshold Eve noticed a sudden movement out of the corner of her eye. She paused and took a closer look. There was something curled up in a dark nook to the right of the doorway. The mark of the dragon on her hand tingled.

'Hello?' Eve asked in a low voice. She took a step forward and halted abruptly. Her eyes adjusted to the darkness of the corner and she realised as she looked up and down

that she was staring at a winged reptile that spanned the full height from floor to ceiling.

A dragon.

Eve held up her trembling palm to show the mark. 'I mean you no harm,' she whispered. The creature's green eyes flashed and it snorted. Despite its terrifying appearance Eve realised that the dragon was as scared as she was.

'I'm here to help you,' Eve continued in a low voice.

The dragon stomped a sharply taloned claw on the stone floor and Eve was stunned at the size of it. She realised the creature was trying to communicate with her. 'I don't understand ... dragon,' she said lamely.

A small rush of flame shot out of the dragon's nostrils. Eve let out a cry and jumped sideways in fright.

'What is it?' Oscar burst through the

doorway and stopped short when he saw the dragon.

'Aha!' he shouted, holding out his hands in a fighting stance.

'No, Oscar!' Eve cried. 'You'll scare it!'

But the dragon had already reared up, its enormous wingspan cramped by the narrow space.

'It's okay,' Eve soothed, but the creature let out a high-pitched shriek and took off out of the open doorway in a rush of wings and talons.

'Quick!' Eve shouted as they ran after it. Outside it took a moment for their eyes to adjust to the bright light.

'Wait!' Eve called but the shadow of the huge creature fell across their faces as it took off in flight.

*E*ve and Oscar followed on foot as fast as they could but the dragon became a small black speck before it disappeared behind a mountain range in the distance.

Eve tried to communicate with the dragon but it didn't answer. They finally stopped running.

'It's hopeless,' Eve panted.

The landscape was mountainous and it was tough going. They were both still thirsty from the fire.

'We should find water before we do anything else,' Oscar decided. 'From the top of that hill we can get a better view.'

The terrain was stony but that made it easier to walk over and in no time they had picked their way to the top of the nearest rise.

'Hills and more hills,' Oscar stated.

Sure enough, a beautiful view of rolling green hills welcomed them. The green became more patchy as the rocky outcrops grew in size. A huge ring of mountains surrounded them.

'What's that?' Eve pointed to a twist of smoke winding into the air.

'More fire,' said Oscar dismally.

The pair climbed three more rises before

they could see clearly what was causing the smoke. It looked like a village market. As they made their way closer Eve could see people selling vegetables and loaves of bread. The smoke was caused by a huge stone oven where fresh loaves of flat bread were being baked. It smelled delicious.

'Yummo!' Oscar inhaled deeply. 'I wonder if they can make me a pizza.'

Eve and Oscar entered the marketplace.

The people selling goods in the market were dressed simply in rough cotton tunics but it was the shoppers who caught Eve's attention. The women wore beautiful, elaborate silk dresses in bright colours. The dresses were long and their hems brushed against the ground. Each woman was heavily accessorised in beads and layers of silver jewellery. But it wasn't only the women who were elegantly dressed. Eve noticed two men

clad in shining metal armour and orange robes. They looked a little like ancient knights but with a distinctive country flair.

Besides the food being sold there were entertainers in the market. They could hear the steady rhythm of drums beating and a flute played a lively tune. Eve noticed a juggler amusing a small group of children who shrieked when all of the balls fell down around them.

Eve caught snippets of conversations and realised she could understand what people were saying. They spoke English but with a thick accent she did not recognise. People stared at Eve and Oscar but when they reached the middle of the crowd nobody gave them a second glance. In fact the stallholders were very friendly. All too soon Eve and Oscar were munching on warm, freshly baked bread dripping with rich butter.

In the distance an elaborate carriage drawn by two horses snaked its way down the hill towards the market. Eve nudged Oscar, who had finished his bread and was eating a delicious-looking vegetable pie. He followed Eve's gaze, raised an eyebrow and kept eating.

As the carriage drew closer the bustle and noise of the market slowly died down. The music stopped and soon the chatter of the people petered out. Everybody stopped what they were doing and stared at the approaching carriage.

'Weird,' Oscar noted, his mouth still full.

The crowd fell completely silent as the carriage entered the marketplace and drew to a halt right in front of Oscar and Eve.

The friends stood up and warily watched the billowing purple material that surrounded the carriage. Two horseriders behind the carriage stopped on either side.

One of the men dismounted and pulled aside the drapes. Inside the carriage Eve could see a woman. She was dressed in purple robes, with gold jewellery around her neck and a simple gold tiara on her head.

The woman turned to look at Eve. 'I am Queen Althea.' She gave a small bow of her head as she addressed the friends.

'I am Eve and this is Oscar,' said Eve, then added, 'Your Majesty' and curtsied. Oscar caught on and gave an awkward bow.

'Come inside and join me.' The queen gestured with her slender hand for Eve to enter the carriage. 'And your friend too,' she added.

Eve hesitated and looked at Oscar for guidance. He shrugged. They knew nothing about Xeria except what Sylvie had said. Eve was mindful of the danger and unsure who she should trust.

'Hurry!' said the queen, more firmly this time. 'There is much to talk about. I have been waiting for you a long time, Eve. Show me your palm.'

How did she know about the magic? Eve reluctantly opened her hand to reveal the mark of the dragon.

'As I thought,' said Althea, looking relieved. Her expression softened. 'Oh, Eve, you can't imagine how awful it has been. So many of our dragons have died.'

Eve sucked in her breath. 'We are here to help,' she said as she stepped into the carriage.

Althea patted the seat next to her. 'Sit with me.'

Eve took the seat next to the queen. Oscar sat opposite. The carriage jerked as it began to move again and soon they were bobbing along with the unfamiliar rhythm of horse-

drawn transport.

'I have a feeling we are going to be fast friends.' Althea took Eve's hand and traced the mark of the dragon with her index finger. The queen's hands were smooth and soft.

Eve smiled and felt for the first time since Sylvie had gone missing that maybe everything was going to be okay.

ve stole a glance at the queen as the carriage bounced along the road. She was very beautiful, with steel-blue eyes and long eyelashes. Her spiky blonde hair was cut short in a pixie cut. She looked younger than Eve's mother but it was hard to pinpoint her age exactly.

What really held Eve's attention was the dragon pendant that Althea wore around

her neck. It was gold like the rest of her jewellery, with a small blue stone that matched the colours of the queen's eyes.

'You like my pendant?' the queen asked.

Eve nodded. The queen held the pendant in her hand as she spoke. 'The dragon is a creature very dear to me but they are nearly lost to us.'

'What do you mean?' asked Eve.

'There is only one dragon left in the whole of Xeria.'

Eve glanced at Oscar. They had seen the last dragon and lost it again! 'What is it?' the queen asked.

'We saw the dragon,' Eve replied.

Althea sat up, her eyes wide with excitement. 'It is alive! There is still time.'

'We lost it,' Eve admitted. 'It flew towards the mountain range.'

But Althea refused to be discouraged.

'I had a feeling about you. You *are* special. Our prayers have been answered. Perhaps now the dragons have a chance of survival.'

'Why are they dying?' Eve asked.

'Did your grandmother not tell you?' The queen sounded surprised.

Eve shook her head. 'You know my gran?'

'We were very close when she came here a long time ago. But there is a man with a dark magic.'

Eve nodded. 'She mentioned the dark magic …'

'His name is Kian. He is a dragon slayer.'

Oscar's ears pricked up. 'A real dragon slayer?' Oscar had read stories about dragon slayers and had recounted their adventures to Eve. They were often portrayed as heroes but Eve and Oscar had agreed that they sounded cruel and cowardly.

'He lives at the base of the volcano where

the dragons once lived. His house is full of trophies from his cruel and wicked killings. Everyone in Xeria lives in fear of him.'

'Why can't you just stop him?' asked Eve.

Althea looked pained. 'His magic is too strong. It was too strong for Sylvie. But you being here gives us hope, Eve.'

Eve thought of the frightened dragon they had seen. It was terrifying but beautiful, and it had not harmed them. How could anyone want to hurt it? Kian had to be stopped.

Eve nodded her head vigorously. 'We will help you.'

Althea smiled. 'He is not easy to find, believe me. He has been hiding out. But if you saw the dragon heading for the mountains I think I know where Kian has gone.'

Oscar was just as sure. 'I scared the dragon away. We need to help.'

Althea pressed her hand into Eve's and held on tightly. 'I only hope we can get to the dragon before Kian does. I know you can do it, Eve. You'll make up for what your grandmother couldn't manage to do. You will save us.'

Eve tried to quell the butterflies in her stomach. She wanted to help the dragon and Althea but she was worried. If Sylvie couldn't defeat the dragon slayer, what hope did she and Oscar have?

'Whoa. A mega mansion!' Oscar exclaimed as he peered out of a gap in the drapes.

Eve stuck her head out of the carriage and looked. There was a large stone castle ahead. It was like something out of a history book or a fairytale. It was tall and imposing, with pointed turrets and flags fluttering in the breeze.

The carriage turned and they entered the castle grounds through an impressive arched entranceway. The surrounding gardens were immaculately tended, with a perfectly trimmed lawn, colourful flowerbeds and fruit trees. Eve could even see horses grazing in the paddocks next to the castle.

'That is my home,' said Althea proudly. 'Welcome to Howlin Castle.'

'It's beautiful,' said Eve.

'It's *very* cool!' Oscar was deeply impressed. 'I always fancied living in a castle.'

The carriage rolled over a real drawbridge towards the entrance.

'Tonight your dream comes true!' Althea clapped her hands together so excitedly that Eve wondered if she was lonely. 'We'll spend the night here and leave early in the morning for the mountains.'

38

Dinner was simple – roasted meats, potatoes and an array of vegetables Eve and Oscar had never seen before. They tasted delicious. Nobody did much talking. Eve and Oscar were seated as guests of honour at either end of a large rectangular dining table with Althea seated between them. Eve found she needed to raise her voice in order to be heard. She was relieved when Althea asked if they were ready to see their rooms. She felt very tired.

The castle really was enormous. Althea led them through seemingly endless corridors before bringing them before two closed doors opposite each other.

'This is your room, Eve. I hope you like it.' Althea pointed to the other door. 'And yours is here, Oscar.'

'I'm glad you know where we are,' Oscar joked. 'I'm completely lost.'

'And tired,' Eve yawned.

Althea gave Eve a light kiss on the cheek. 'Sleep well. I'll wake you both early. We'll leave at dawn.'

Eve and Oscar stood side by side and watched Althea glide away.

'What a strange place to grow up in,' Eve commented.

'Sort of spooky,' Oscar agreed. He yawned and opened the door to his room. 'See you in the morning.'

Eve opened her own elaborately carved wooden door and went inside. On one side of the room was a four-poster bed made up with pale pink silk sheets. The rest of the room was simple, with books, a dressing table and a painting of a dragon hung on the wall opposite.

'I do feel like a princess,' Eve thought sleepily. She didn't even bother to undress

but sank onto the mattress. The pillows were luxuriously soft and the bed very inviting.

Eve curled up and looked out the window. As night set in she had a clear view of the tallest mountain. It looked ominous, its dark presence watching her. She smiled as she listened to Oscar mucking about with a sword in the next room. Her last thought was *Typical boy!* – and then she promptly fell asleep.

***

As she had promised, Althea woke Eve while it was still dark outside. She was dressed very differently. Gone were her purple silk robes. Instead she wore a simple cream tunic underneath a leather bodice.

'The bodice keeps us warm and also acts as armour,' she explained when she saw Eve studying it.

Althea brought Eve and Oscar some supplies. They were each given a small backpack with water, food and spare clothes. On Althea's instruction they changed out of their regular clothes and dressed in similar light tunics, with a leather bodice for Eve and a vest for Oscar. They were also fitted with sturdy black leather boots.

'Now you look ready,' Althea nodded. 'You can get all kinds of weather in the mountains. Best to be prepared.'

It was just getting light as the trio set off up a narrow track along the base of the mountain. Althea seemed happy to join Eve and Oscar without any of her guards. She took the lead and set a good pace. It was very pretty countryside, with lots of wildflowers, streams and little waterfalls.

Eve breathed in the fresh mountain air as she walked, but Althea's long strides soon

made it difficult to keep up and Eve found that her breathing was laboured. But time passed quickly and soon it was time for a drink break.

'Xeria is really beautiful,' Eve said as she took a swig of water from the leather pouch attached to her backpack.

'Thank you,' said Althea. 'But ruling a kingdom is not easy.'

'Why is the dragon so important to Xeria?' Oscar asked.

'It's a symbol of strength for us. Dragons are the most amazing creatures. They roam free and cannot be tamed. They possess a very powerful magic.'

'Good thing you are trying to protect them,' Eve noted. 'In our world there are still poachers who kill animals for their body parts. It's horrible.'

'We should keep moving.' Althea busily

packed up their snacks. 'We have a tough climb ahead of us.'

'How far are we going?' Oscar asked, looking up at the steep sides of the mountain ahead.

'To the top, silly!' Althea laughed, shaking her head.

Oscar groaned. 'I had a feeling you were going to say that.'

'We need to be tied together now, just in case one of us slips.' Althea stopped and wound strong rope around their waists, linking them together. She led the way, with Eve in the middle and Oscar bringing up the rear, as they slowly made their way up the rock face.

The walking was hard going. The track grew so steep that they began to climb over the rocks. Then the path ended and the only way to continue to the top was to pick their

way slowly along a narrow rock ledge.

'You're nearly there,' Althea called back as she lifted herself off the ledge and out of sight.

'Whatever you do, don't look down!' Eve reminded Oscar.

Oscar nodded and then sneaked a look at the drop below. 'Too late,' he groaned. 'I don't feel so good ...' Eve saw him begin to sway.

'What's wrong?' Althea called and tugged on the rope.

'Oscar's afraid of heights.' Eve stretched out a hand to steady Oscar but before she reached him his eyes closed and he fell backwards.

His weight jerked Eve to the ground and her body slid over the loose rocks. She grabbed a protruding rock to stop herself.

'Althea!' Eve cried through gritted teeth

as her fingers began to slip. 'I can't hold on!'

Oscar had fainted. He was hanging freely in the air, suspended only by the rope around Eve's waist.

$\mathcal{E}$ve focused as hard as she could on gripping the rock. Her fingers ached with the strain and her shoulders throbbed.

'Just hold on while I anchor the main rope to something.' Althea hurried to untie her own rope. 'I'm not strong enough to hold both of you.'

Eve felt her hands slipping on the rough

surface. 'Hurry!' she urged.

'There's a tree trunk just above us. Don't move, Eve,' Althea said and disappeared from view. Eve felt a sharp tug on the rope, then Althea reappeared on the rock ledge.

'Let's hope that holds.' Althea grasped the rope and inched her way towards Eve. 'Hold on, Eve, I'm nearly there.'

Too late Eve felt her fingers slipping and the pain grew too much. All of a sudden she was falling. The ground gave way and Eve screamed.

'Eve!' Althea cried and tried to grab her.

Eve felt the rope around her middle grow taut and suddenly she was dangling. She opened her eyes and realised she was suspended in the air. The rope tied to the tree trunk had held. Eve looked down. Oscar was still hanging below her, his shoulders slumped.

'Althea!' Eve called.

'I'm trying, Eve!' Althea tried to pull in the rope but with two bodies weighing it down it was too heavy for her.

'Try swinging the rope and I'll see if I can grab hold of a rock,' Eve shouted. Perhaps with some momentum she could get hold of something. She resisted the urge to look down.

Althea took the hanging rope in both hands and started to swing it back and forth. At first Eve barely moved but slowly the rope gained momentum. With each swing Eve and Oscar moved closer to the rocks and then away again. Each time Eve tried to lunge for a rock she missed.

Althea moved as close to Eve as she dared. She reached out a hand into the air and, as the rope swung towards her, just managed to grab hold of Eve's hand. Eve gripped

Althea with all of her strength.

'Let's get off this cliff face,' muttered Althea.

The two girls managed to reel in the rope that held Oscar. Althea dragged Eve up to the safety of the stony plateau at the top of the mountain and together they heaved Oscar onto the level ground. The girls sank back against the large tree.

'That was too close for comfort.' Eve let out a huge sigh. Her hands were still shaking and she felt like vomiting.

'You're telling me,' agreed Althea. 'Why didn't I bring my guards with us?'

Oscar's eyes fluttered open. 'What happened?' he asked groggily as he sat up and took in his surroundings.

Althea began to giggle. Oscar looked at her in confusion. Then Eve joined in. She couldn't help it. Soon they were in fits of laughter, tears streaming down their faces.

'What?' Oscar was even more bemused. He stood up uncertainly and looked out over the edge.

'Don't look down!' Eve yelled and grabbed him by the ankle to restrain him.

'Okay!' Oscar shook his leg free. 'I'm going to look around if that's okay with you two?'

This set off another round of giggling. Oscar shook his head at the pair of them.

As Oscar slowly walked around the bare rock plateau, Eve took in their surroundings. There was very little vegetation except for sparse grass and the odd clump of wildflowers. The area was very flat.

'Hey, Eve!' Oscar called. 'This isn't a mountain – it's a volcano!' Eve moved over to the middle of the plateau. The hole Oscar was staring at was the volcano's crater.

'We call it the fire god,' said Althea as she joined them.

'We learned about volcanoes at school,' Oscar declared. 'I remember reading that the soil around volcanoes is rich from the volcanic loam.'

'This is why Xeria is so fertile, why our farming is so good,' Althea explained. 'But we have to keep the fire god happy or it gets angry.'

'How do you keep it happy?' Oscar asked.

'We make offerings,' Althea smiled. 'Everyone likes getting presents, don't they?'

Eve felt a chill run through her body. It was cold at the summit of the mountain. She rubbed her arms to get her circulation going. All of a sudden she felt a sharp pain in her chest.

'Ah,' she gasped and doubled over.

'What is it?' Oscar was next to her in a flash.

Eve gripped her side. Her body was racked

with cramps and sharp shooting pains.

'My hand ...' Eve held out her palm. The mark of the dragon was an angry red welt on her skin. Her hand throbbed painfully. 'The dragon is here.'

'Where?' Oscar gestured to the flat land at the summit of the mountain.

'It's hiding in the crater of the volcano.' She grimaced again.

Althea beamed. 'I knew you would find it, Eve! I knew you would help me find the last dragon.'

'Not if I have anything to do with it,' said a deep male voice.

Althea's eyes narrowed. Eve swung around to see a young man stepping out from behind a large boulder.

'Hello, Kian.' Althea spat the words out with venom. 'Eve and Oscar, meet the dragon slayer.'

'You have a nerve calling *me* a dragon slayer,' Kian sneered at Althea.

Kian took a few steps towards them. He was a tall, muscular young man with a thick mop of red hair. Eve noticed that his face and hands were covered in scars. He wore similar clothes to the villagers they had seen in the market – a tunic and a wide

leather belt – but in one hand he held a large, very sharp-looking sword.

Eve tried to concentrate but the pain in her hand was growing stronger. The dragon was calling to her. It was becoming more and more scared. It was warning her. The dragon slayer had to be stopped.

'You're not going any further,' Kian said in a firm voice. 'This is my mountain and I protect all its creatures.'

Althea snorted. 'If killing innocent creatures is your idea of protection!' she scoffed.

Kian turned to Eve. 'Eve, your magic has led you to the last dragon. If this dragon dies there will be no more. Althea is not to be trusted.'

Eve looked at Kian with disbelief. 'Althea is my friend. She saved my life.'

Kian shook his head. 'Only because she

needed you to find the dragon for her. I doubt she'll need you much longer.'

'Silence!' Althea pointed a finger at Kian and a bolt of fire shot out from her fingertip. It flew straight through the air and hit Kian in the chest. He was flung backwards and landed on the ground.

'What have you done?' Eve cried and ran to the young man's side. Kian was unconscious but still breathing. Oscar stared wild-eyed at Althea, deep in shock.

Althea rolled her eyes. 'I don't have time for this. When you are queen you have to make tough decisions. Kian is a threat to Xeria.'

'Is he dead?' asked Oscar.

Althea shook her head impatiently. 'What of it? He meddled in my affairs.'

'Ah!' Eve cried out in pain and doubled over again, gripping her palm.

'The dragon needs you, Eve,' Althea cried, her eyes lighting up. 'Take us to it!'

'I can't walk …' Eve's body was again filled with pain. Oscar put his arm around Eve and lifted her to stand, then helped her to walk towards the crater. They picked their way carefully among the small rocks and ash. In no time at all they were all covered in soot, their hands and faces blackened.

I'm coming, Eve told the dragon silently. *I'm coming to save you.*

The dragon answered with a squeal that felt like it had pierced Eve's ear. She realised her head also throbbed. She was barely conscious and so weak she could hardly walk. Her skin burned and prickled with the heat. She stumbled over the small rocks until Oscar lifted her into his arms and carried her.

Althea followed close behind but Eve

no longer noticed. All she could see in her mind was the dragon. She saw its shiny grey skin tinged with purple and the scales that shimmered like sequins. She saw its long tail wrapped around its body and its enormous wings lying loosely against its back. Those large cat-like eyes Eve remembered were closed.

Eve's vision cleared and she realised it was no longer an image in her head. She was staring at the dragon. It lay curled up in a small cave. It lifted its head and locked its pale green eyes with hers. She could see that because of its colouring the dragon blended into the rock face. It wouldn't have been found without her magic.

'The last dragon,' Eve whispered.

'At last!' Althea cried. 'You have done well, Eve.'

Eve's head fell back on Oscar's arms and

he kneeled down to better support her. 'Eve? Are you okay? Eve?' Oscar pleaded. 'Speak to me!' He looked at Althea. 'She's ill, Althea. Help her.'

Althea barely glanced in their direction. She only had eyes for the last dragon. 'It doesn't matter to me if she lives or dies.'

'What do you mean?' Oscar asked. 'Eve! Hold on!'

Another chill ran through Eve's body as she watched Althea make her way to the dragon. With a sick feeling she realised they had been wrong to trust Althea.

'It's a trap,' Eve whispered feverishly. 'She used us to get to the dragon. Oscar ... *she's* the dragon slayer.'

Oscar stared in horror at Althea. They could see that the queen's whole manner had changed. She no longer looked friendly; a cold intensity burned in her eyes. Oscar

stood up slowly, picking up a decent-sized rock as he did so.

'Not another step, Althea!' Oscar commanded the queen. 'Leave the dragon alone.'

'Your rock won't stop me, boy.' Althea kept walking, looking straight at the dragon.

Oscar hesitated then threw the rock at Althea with all his might. Without even turning around she sent out a jet of fire that shattered the rock into tiny shards. Oscar ducked to miss the sharp debris. It scattered all over the rocks around them.

'Try that again and it will be *you* in tiny pieces,' she hissed.

'Why are you doing this?' Eve cried out. 'This is evil. You can't just wipe out a species.'

'I've done it before,' Althea declared. 'When this dragon dies I will have eternal power. The dark magic will be mine. The

fire god and I have an agreement. This is my final act.' Althea glanced at Eve. 'You were no challenge to me at all. Now there's nobody left to stop me. You are mine, dragon. All mine.'

The dragon had no strength left to flee, so strong was Althea's magic. It closed its eyes, ready to die.

ve's whole body ached. She was burning up. She felt as if she was back in the fire in the attic. Then she looked up and saw the sky above. It was red.

Eve remembered. The dragon.

She sat up and saw Althea standing over the dragon. They were both bathed in a red light. Was she too late? Fire was streaming from Althea's fingertips.

Eve spoke to the dragon. *I know you're still alive, I can feel it*, she said, struggling to stand. *Don't give up.*

The queen is too strong, the weakened dragon protested. *Her magic is dark.*

Well, my magic is light! Eve was so angry that she was shaking. Althea had tricked her and pretended to be her friend. She had pretended to love dragons and the land and her people. But Althea was a long way from the person Eve had thought she was.

'Help me up, Oscar,' Eve croaked. 'I'm not going down without a fight.' Oscar grabbed her arm and helped her to stand. She steadied herself on the wall of the crater.

Eve took a deep breath, then spoke loudly. 'What happened when my grandmother came here?'

Althea glanced at Eve. 'Your precious grandmother was as stupid as you are!' Her

eyes gleamed at the memory. 'My sacrifices weren't as big in those days. I didn't need as much of the magic. It was the faeries she tried to save.'

'Faeries?'

'Nature spirits.'

'What happened?' Eve channelled all of her energy. She blazed with anger. *Get ready*, she said to the dragon.

'She was here at this moment – just like you, little Eve. She failed to save the last faerie, just as you are about to fail to save the last dragon. She fled the world of Xeria in shame.' Althea shrugged. 'And she's never been back. Your grandmother is a coward.'

Now! Eve called to the dragon. She held out her palm and felt the magic of the dragon race through her veins. Her body burned and from her palm flowed a blue light that she pointed at Althea. At the same

time the dragon let out a stream of fire of its own. The clash of energies sounded like an explosion.

Althea threw back her head and laughed. The magic had absolutely no effect on her.

'Child's magic!' Althea scoffed. 'I've had a power you cannot imagine for centuries.'

Eve kept the light pouring out of her, beaming it onto Althea, but began to feel faint. Althea was right. Eve could barely stand without Oscar's help and the dragon looked completely spent. Althea laughed.

'You're not the only one who has been working on their magic over the years.' A familiar voice broke through Althea's cackle.

Althea spun around. '*You*!'

Eve gasped and grabbed Oscar's arm for support. 'Gran?'

Her grandmother was standing on a rock ledge above them. Kian stood behind her.

Eve noticed Sylvie carried a wooden staff. At its tip was a gleaming crystal the size of an orange.

'Xeria shall be ruled by you no more, Althea.' Sylvie seemed to grow taller and a brilliant blue light shone from the crystal.

Sylvie's magic was strong. Eve felt it flow through her. She pointed her marked palm at Althea and the blue light poured out of her too. The blue pushed back Althea's red flames until her fiery ray petered out to nothing.

'You can't destroy me!' the queen cackled as she leaped up onto another rock closer to the top of the crater. 'You failed again, Sylvie!'

'She's getting away!' called Eve.

'You have great power, Althea. It's true I cannot destroy you, but I won't have to.'

Sylvie raised her staff into the air and

the blue light flooded the crater. Suddenly the sky above the mountain was filled with dragons – huge, terrible dragons, medium-sized dragons, even baby dragons. They swept down into the crater on their enormous black wings. In a chorus of shrieks and growls and hissing they bore down on Althea.

'It seems the dragons are not pleased with what you have been up to.'

'Get away from me!' Althea shrieked as she tried to bat the dragons away. The largest dragon plucked Althea into the air and held her in its talons. With a final beating of wings they flew up and out of the crater with the screaming witch in their clutches.

'I wonder if Althea will like a taste of her own medicine,' Sylvie chuckled.

Eve stared at her grandmother. 'Gran … what are you doing here?'

'Yes, we have much to talk about but right now this dragon needs our help, dear.'

Eve looked over at the dragon. It lay completely still and was no longer breathing.

ve and Sylvie worked through the night trying to heal the dragon. They made hot poultices to heal the open wounds caused by Althea's magic. Sylvie spent a long time muttering spells while rubbing her crystal staff across the dragon's body.

The long night gave Eve a chance to hear Kian's story. Kian had met Sylvie when she

first visited Xeria. Kian and Althea had been best friends when they were little kids. They fell out when he realised that Althea was using evil magic to control the land.

Towards dawn, Sylvie left the dragon sleeping and joined them around the open fire that Kian had built. 'We'll just have to wait and see what the morning brings,' she said, stirring a brew over the fire.

'Is that a magic potion?' Oscar asked.

'I'm making a cup of tea,' Sylvie chuckled. 'It's freezing up here. An old lady needs her creature comforts.'

'How old was Althea really?' Eve asked.

'Hundreds of years old. I met her when I was a girl not much older than you and she hasn't aged a day.'

One by one the dragons returned to the crater to watch over their mate. The biggest was about four times the height of Eve and

its talons were the length of her arm.

'Where have all the dragons been?'

Sylvie poured a cup of steaming tea and sat down with a sigh. 'Ever since Althea wiped out the faeries I have kept an eye on Xeria. When I realised what she was doing to the dragons I hid them in other worlds.'

'You can do that?' Oscar asked.

Sylvie shrugged. 'My job is to protect the creatures who need me.' She blew on the tea to cool it. 'I left this one here as bait with Kian watching over him. Althea had to be caught in the act.'

Eve's brow creased. 'Why couldn't you have come with me and we could have fought Althea together?'

Sylvie took a sip of tea. 'I was worried that Althea would try to destroy you or use you against me. As she needed you, she would keep you alive. It was a gamble, but the life

of a crystal keeper is full of risk, Eve.'

Eve understood.

'I also needed to see for myself if Ingvar was your kindred animal.'

'Ingvar?'

'The last dragon.' Sylvie looked over at the sleeping dragon. 'All crystal keepers have a kindred animal. Ingvar is yours.'

'Mine?' Eve's eyes grew round. She glanced over at the sleeping dragon.

'Cool!' Oscar added.

'As soon as he's well enough to travel he's coming back home with us.'

Eve gaped. 'But he's a *dragon*!'

Sylvie chuckled. 'There are many things ordinary people do not see in our world. But they are there. You just need to know how to look for them.'

'Do you have a kindred animal?' Oscar asked.

'Of course.' Sylvie stood up and threw the dregs of her tea into the fire. The flames hissed quietly. Oscar and Eve stared at each other, stunned. Eve was bursting with questions. Sylvie saw her expression and chuckled.

'Hush now. You'll find out everything in good time. Now I need to check on the patient.' Sylvie slowly walked over to where Ingvar slept.

'A dragon?' Eve mouthed at Oscar.

'A dragon!' Oscar's eyes shined.

***

After a week of rest and fattening up, Ingvar was well enough to travel. It was hard for Eve to say goodbye to Kian and the dragons they had come to know and love. Oscar in particular was sad as he had been spending

most of his time riding dragons across Xeria with Kian, checking on the world.

'Come back soon?' Kian asked, giving Eve a brisk hug.

'I will.'

'Ready?' Sylvie asked Eve.

'Ready,' Eve replied.

'You have much to learn, Eve. Our world will look very different to you when you return. You will be able to see many creatures you couldn't see before. But with knowledge comes responsibility. When we get back your training with Ingvar begins in earnest. There is a lot to do.'

'And Oscar?' Eve asked.

Sylvie smiled. 'I have many plans for Oscar. We need him. You need him.'

Eve nodded. She looked down at the dragon she and Oscar were riding. 'Ready, Ingvar?'

Ingvar answered with a snort. A burst of flames shot out of his mouth. Eve grabbed hold of Ingvar's neck and braced herself for the fall. She closed her eyes, knowing that when she next opened them she would be home.

ABOUT THE AUTHOR

Jess Black enjoys writing stories with heaps of action and humour. She has previously co-written *The Bindi Wildlife Adventure Series*, a fictional series about helping endangered animals around the world.

Now available in the series

KEEPER OF THE CRYSTALS

Eve and the Runaway Unicorn

JESS BLACK

KEEPER OF THE CRYSTALS

Eve and the Fiery Phoenix

JESS BLACK

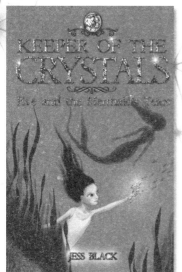

KEEPER OF THE CRYSTALS

Eve and the Mermaids' Tears

JESS BLACK

KEEPER OF THE CRYSTALS

Eve and the Lost Dragon

JESS BLACK

For more riddles and
adventures visit
www.keeperofthecrystals.com.au